Leave nothing but footprints

Copyright © (Caroline Nieuwenhuis 2020)

ISBN: 978-178456-689-0

Perfect Bound

First published 2020 by UPFRONT PUBLISHING
Peterborough, England.

An environmentally friendly book printed and bound in England
by www.printondemand-worldwide.com

For each and every person who donated towards my Crowdfunding campaign to bring my story to life!

"Cherish the natural world, because you're a part of it and you depend on it."
~ Sir David Attenborough

The sun is up and the birds
are singing, a great day to unwind.
Let's dive down to the ocean floor,
to see what friends we can find!

Hey there, little turtle!
How are you doing?
What's wrong with your tum?
You're normally playing
around the coral,
laughing, having fun!

I thought these were some jellyfish,
my favourite type of food, but
now I've gone and eaten one,
I don't feel so good!

Oh no, that's bad!
Can I help at all?
I think it might be plastic!
How do they end up
in the sea?
We must do
something drastic!

Humans leave them
on the beach,
it makes it
such a mess.
One thing you can
do to help, is be sure
to use them less!

Good morning crab,
what's your news today?
You look a little
confused!
Can I answer
any questions?
So you don't
feel bemused?

My home was getting a little tight, so I found myself a new shell, but something doesn't feel quite right, what's wrong, can you tell?

I think you've made a mistake, my
friend, it hasn't gone to plan.
For what you thought was a shiny
new shell, is actually a drinks can!

Oh dear, silly me! What a mistake!
There's one thing that I wish, for
people to clean up after themselves,
and not leave it for the fish!

Hello whale, why are you so glum?
There's no smile on your face!
Maybe a lovely song will help,
would that be the case?

Plankton is my favourite meal,
it really is a treat, but when
I search around for some,
plastic is all I find to eat!

That's terrible news, no good at all, a matter we can't ignore! Where has all this come from, the waves to the ocean floor?

If there weren't so many bottles around, it would be much easier to see, for I could eat whatever I want, and live life wild and free!

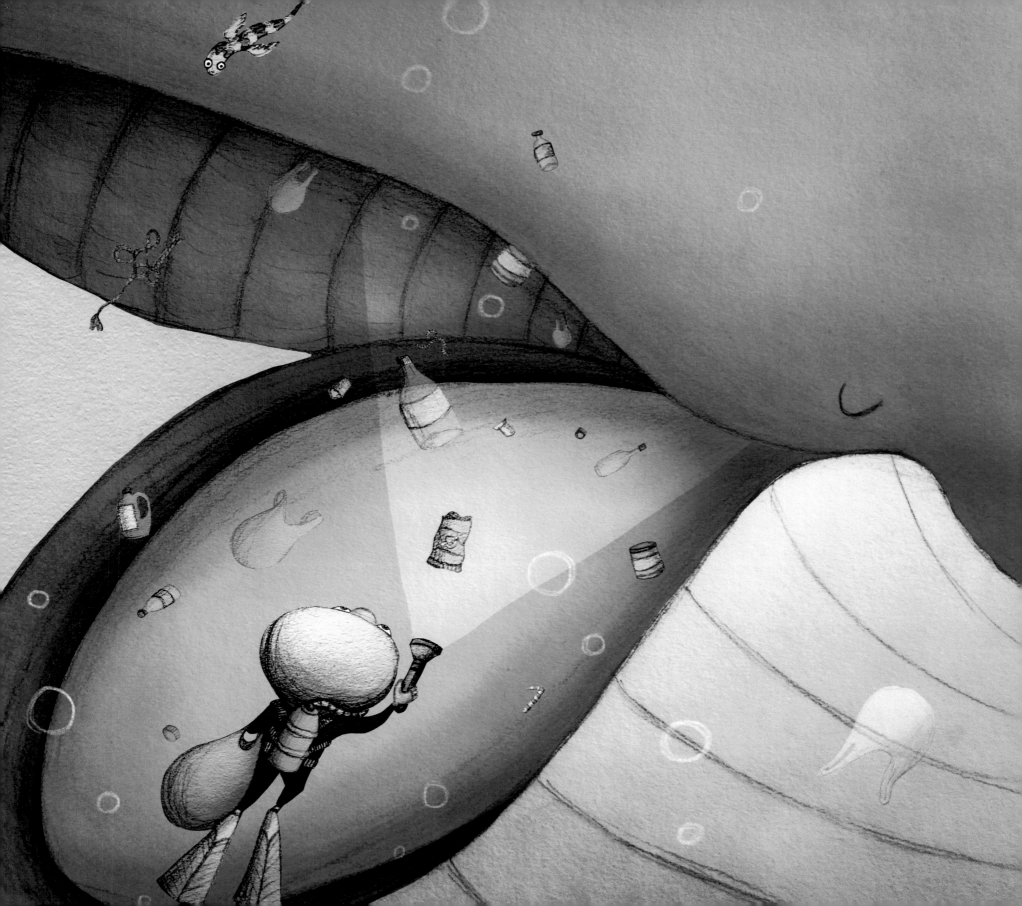

Afternoon seal, are you enjoying the sun? It's such a beautiful day! Maybe we can paddle together, joke around and play?

I love to swim in circles, and dive among the wrecks, but yesterday I was splashing around, and got something stuck on my neck!

That looks to me like a plastic toy,
I think it's called a frisbee,
but how did it end up on the beach,
and floating out to sea?

People leave them when it's time to go
home, after enjoying a nice day,
what would make it better for us,
is if they always took them away!

Puffer fish
I came as quick
as I could, after hearing
a lot of commotion! I thought
I'd find you hiding under
a rock, not in the middle
of the ocean!

Hello there, what a relief you're here! There seems to be an issue! For every time I take a breath...

Oh no, that's bad! I'd be happy to help!
Your nose looks awfully sore!
I think I see what's causing it,
a little plastic straw!

This isn't the first time it's happened to
me, if only people would think, how
straws end up washed into the ocean,
each time they finish their drink!

It seems that plastic has become a big problem, but there must be a simple solution? What can we humans do to help stop this plastic pollution?

It's all about making little changes, a small difference here and there, and start to show the ocean creatures that we all really do care!

If we can work together,
it's down to you and me,
to think before we use each day,
to keep plastic out of the sea!

The most important lesson for us,
is to give each other hints,
and remember when we visit the beach,
to leave nothing but footprints!

RE - #0002 - 150321 - C29 - 250/280/2 - PB - 9781784566890 - Gloss Lamination